CHALLENGE FROM BEYOND

They call themselves the Sukhi—if they had mouths with which to form words or had any need of a label at all. But labels are necessary when dealing with primitive beings and also, perhaps, it was an indulgence to the need of personal identification. The ego which can only be expressed as something unique.

Or, again, it could have been only a part of the game they were playing.

"Call us the Sukhi. What and who we are and from where we came need not concern you, but you may think of us as two, as male and female. Balik and Avura, such small details will amuse you as the game will amuse you. A simple game based on the basic elements of life itself and incorporating a jest of a delicate nature. Only the strong deserve to survive therefore prove your worth or vanish from the face of the cosmos!"

GREGORY KERN is one of the world's greatest masters of the interplanetary adventure novel. His novels of danger between the stars and exotic adventure on strange worlds have been published in millions of copies throughout the world. They will be found not only in the United States and Canada, but also in Great Britain, Australia, New Zealand, and wherever English is read.

DAW Books by Gregory Kern include:

BEYOND THE GALACTIC LENS
A WORLD AFLAME
MIMICS OF DEPHENE
THE GHOSTS OF EPIDORUS
and many others.

The Galactiad

Gregory Kern

DAW BOOKS, INC.

DONALD A. WOLLHEIM, PUBLISHER

1633 Broadway, New York, NY 10019

FIRST PRINTING, JULY 1983

1 2 3 4 5 6 7 8 9

 DAW TRADEMARK REGISTERED
U.S. PAT. OFF. MARCA
REGISTRADA. HECHO EN U.S.A.

PRINTED IN U.S.A.

CHAPTER
ONE

Commander Breson woke at the first note of the alarm, rolling from his bed and into his uniform, dressing with trained speed, pausing only to dash a handful of water into his face, swallowing another as he ran from his cabin.

As he burst into the operations room, Major Piazzoni looked up from his desk and said, quietly, "Zero plus 36, sir."

Over half a minute to wake, get dressed, get to his station. Not bad, but not good enough. Breson had set himself a half-minute maximum—those extra six seconds would be a later cause of worry. Not that it mattered, the duty-crew would have done all that was necessary, but no one with his responsibility could afford to be lenient with himself.

Curtly, Breson said, "Report?"

"Auxiliary vessels moving into intercept positions, sir. Reserves manned and leaving."

"Time?"

Piazzoni glanced at his panel. "Zero plus 42."

"Too long!" Breson's voice reflected his anger. "Those stand-by crews are getting slack. Make a note to double all drills. I want them to be aboard and free within half a minute."

"Noted, sir." Major Piazzoni glanced at Captain Renato and lifted his eyebrow a fraction. The Old Man was prickly and it was a time to tread softly. With relief he saw the flash of tell-tales on his consol. "All stations battle-manned, sir."

"Time?"

Breson relaxed a little as he heard it. He was a short, thick-set man with muscles which bulked his trim uniform of blue and green and silver. His face was ruddy, the cheeks seamed with a mass of tiny lines, more lines etching the corners of his eyes. His mouth was hard, the lips thin, the jaw determined. A man who had earned his rank and position and who intended that his command should be better than any other MALACA; faster, more efficient, more tautly trained.

"Enemy?"

"Fifteen units approaching from the eighth decant, five from the third. More on scattered intercept paths. A blanket attack which I guess is to serve as a diversion to enable the main force to bypass our attack-potential."

"You guess, mister?"

Major Piazzoni flinched at the acid comment.

"Sorry, sir. I assume."

"You could be assuming too much." Breson strode across the room to the main screens. They were alive with glowing colors, points of red and blue, yellow and emerald, white and orange. The thin lines of noted and extrapolated positions made a skein against the steady points of distant stars, the fuzz of distant nebulae.

Too much detail for any man to fully comprehend, but the computers would take care of the essentials, Breson wanted only the general pattern.

Adding his own intuition to the mechanical efficiency of the machines.

"Send units to position 875924," he rapped. "Class-two vessels—an entire squad."

"Divert them, sir?"

"Use the reserves." Breson knew he could be wrong, his hunch at fault, but the attackers had managed to open a gap through which the mother ship itself could be attacked. He added, "Adopt evasive procedure. Random shifts."

At the boards men relayed the commands, lights winking, instruments recording the activity inside the great vessel, the constantly changing position. A ship which held ships and men and machines; tools with which to rehabilitate a world, energies sufficient to destroy suns.

Breson could feel it as he stood before the screens, the very metal of his command seeming to become a physical part of him, the mighty engines the pulse of his heart, the computers the mesh of his brain, the auxiliary vessels, now far distant, extensions of his fingers, his hands.

If those ships were to be destroyed he would feel the pain, the loss, the seething rage of something which had been wantonly hurt.

And, hurt, he would kill.

As every MALACA in space would kill if Earth or its affiliated worlds, which formed the Terran Sphere, should be threatened by any hostile force.

One day it would come, he thought bleakly. An ambitious race led by a power-hungry ruler would embark on a suicidal path of attempted conquest. Ships and the fury of atomic destruction would be aimed against peaceful worlds and the delicate balance of the *Pax Terra* sundered.

A race or combine of races trying to do by force what they had failed to do by guile.

Trying—and failing.

If the shields of the MALACAs could be kept strong, if the sword they held poised over any invader could be kept honed to a fine edge.

"Units in position, sir." Major Piazzoni's voice was flat, emotionless. "Seven interceptors lost. Nine others damaged and unoperational."

"The enemy?"

"Twenty-eight units destroyed."

A fair exchange, but not good enough. As yet the conflict had been far distant, scouts intercepting the enemy and doing their job, men, technically dying, blood and guts spilled into the void, their vessels turned into glowing masses of radiant vapor or ripped open to drift helplessly in space.

They would die if this had been real and not a simulated exercise.

"Engage all reserves," rapped Breson. "Triple layer of interceptors. Plot origin of attack and launch a counter-offensive. Move!"

He was matching his skill and intuition against the

secret programming devised by the experts on Earth. A test which had been triggered by remote control and one he would meet or be replaced. If he failed then it would be the end of his active career; an early retirement or to take up a position in a training academy to teach youngsters who now itched to fill his shoes.

That fact he accepted—Earth could not afford to be defended by anything less than the best.

The second wave came, simulated ships hurtling through the void, the computers checking and assessing each defensive maneuver, adding gains and losses, ships taken out, fire-power diminished, potential damage noted. A make-believe battle which would take hours and strain every nerve and sinew to the uttermost.

To Breson it was real.

To Lieutenant Edward Sharrat it was not.

He sat at the controls of his three-man interceptor and glowered at the screens. Even the thrill and test of a simulated battle would have been better than maintaining a holding position in an area which all sense and logic told him would remain empty of possible targets. And there was little fun in tracking down a computerized point on the screens, of firing empty guns and aiming nonexistent torpedoes.

"We're stuck," he said disgustedly. "No high points for us, no big scores. Just come out, wait, then go back to listen to the boasting. Can you imagine what Hardy will say? Fifteen kills and not a scratched plate. Soon he'll make captain."

"Maybe." Fahey relaxed in his turret. "Me, I just take things as they come. Show me a target and I'll get it. Show me empty space and I'm grateful. Who wants to get killed?"

"No one." At the engines Walcott checked a dial. "But you're all noise, Fahey. When it comes to the crunch you'll be just as much a hero as the rest. You too, Lieutenant."

"Just give me the chance." Automatically Sharrat checked his screens. His vessel was one of a group of three, occupying the lowest point of a triangle. Above and to either side rode the ships of Lieutenants Raynor and Mignon. They, he guessed, were as disgruntled as himself.

"You know," he said musingly, "the last time I saw real action was on Aieda. That was when the Regent asked for aid. He wanted to cut a channel between the Elgarth Ocean and the Illmert Sea. Remember?"

"I remember." Walcott was short. "I lost a buddy to the Qraik."

"What about that time on Lekhard?" Fahey moved a little to stay alert.

"That was just a reclaiming job—I'm talking about action. We hit a Qraik nest and all hell hit us for a while. Right, Sergeant?"

"Right," said Walcott. "Ten good men lost in the first attack. Fifteen more captured and what those things did to them doesn't bear telling. We had to use atomics in the end."

"Aieda," said Fahey. "I wasn't in on that one." He sounded regretful. "But it just goes to show that life is full of surprises."

That scrap of philosophy Sharrat could have done without. He settled back, a portion of his mind on the screen, trained reflexes ready for action should it be needed. Not that it would. All these exercises were basically alike, and no matter how much they tried to make it appear the real thing, something was lacking. Not because of fore knowledge—the alarm caught everyone on the hop with maybe the exception of the commander himself, though rumor had it he took no advantage—but because of the conviction that no matter what the computers said no one would really get hurt.

A war in which no one risked anything was hard to take seriously.

The lieutenant was young, age would bring wisdom, the realization that armed might was to prevent, not to indulge in conflict. That the toasts offered and drunk in the senior ward rooms had real meaning.

"To peace—long may it last!"

A light winked on the consol and he checked it, suddenly fully alert, but it was nothing more than a signal picked up from some natural spatial phenomena. A cluster of dying atoms, an electro-gravitic vortex which had come into being only to suddenly vanish. The void was full of such minor distortions.

For a moment he was tempted to check with the others of the group, but decided against it. Idle chatter was frowned on during battle-alert.

It came again and the speaker came to life.

"Sharrat, did you see it?" Raynor, sounding anxious. "A register on the Larvic-Shaw."

"I caught it—probably a local distortion."

"We'd better triangulate." Mignon, older than the others, long overdue for promotion and a little worried that he was still a junior officer. "My guess is that it came from a point just a little ahead. Maybe a new weapon of some kind."

A remote possibility, but it could be a test, a challenge to their awareness. Sharrat leaned forward and adjusted the instruments. The Larvic-Shaw Spatial Disturbance Detector could register the presence of any mass or energy vortex of a low order. He studied the even flow of lines across the screen.

"Nothing," he reported. "It seems all clear now. Raynor?"

"The same."

"How about you, Mignon?"

"Negative, but maybe we should report it."

A doubt which immediately betrayed why he had not received his promotion. Mignon was the senior; the responsibility was his, as was the decision.

He said, weakly, "It could be nothing. We don't want to start a false alarm but—" His voice broke, resumed with a shout. "Dear God! What's that?"

It had appeared from nothing. One second space was empty, the next a great glowing ball of lambent orange stood before them. A ball which pulsed and writhed as if alive.

"The size!" Mignon was babbling. "It's—"

The voice died, suddenly, cut as if with a knife, but it was no knife. A thin streak of orange had shot from the writhing ball, had touched the vessel in which he rode—and then there was nothing.

No ship.

No register of any kind.

Complete and utter annihilation.

"God!" Sharrat's hands leapt to the controls. "Raynor!"

A warning which, if needed, came too late. Again came the thread of orange but this time there was no annihilation. Instead the small vessel jerked as if gripped by tremendous forces. The nose opened, peeled back as if the hull had been the skin of a banana, a litter of debris spilling into the void. Small things, loose articles, a suit, a heap of rations, the bodies of three men.

Men already dead, their mouths open, ringed with blood from their ruptured lungs.

Corpses which the orange glow embraced.

"Fahey! The guns!"

The interceptor moved as Sharrat hit the controls, the pulse of the engine rising to a thin whine, the hull quivering from transmitted vibrations. From the turret came the sound of cursing as the gunner ripped free the monitoring connections and fed torpedoes into their launchers.

"Fire, damn you!" Sharrat tripped the radio-switch and engaged the automatic sender to the mother-ship. "Fire!"

Fahey was good. He ignored the wrecked vessel now falling away, concentrating on the orange ball which retained its original size, eyes narrowed as he aligned the sights, hands tripping the releases.

Slender shapes spat from the launching tubes, hydrive torpedoes fitted with nuclear warheads, each holding massed megatons of compacted energy. They hit true, slamming into the center of the orange ball, vanishing into it like a stone into water.

"Try again." Sharrat flung his little craft through space, long and arduous training eliminating the need for conscious thought. To hit, to run, to dodge and to hit again was the role of an interceptor. To dart in and kill and escape in order to kill again. "Use three-second fuses and cut hydrive."

A risk, but one which had to be taken. The orange ball was too close for tremendous velocity to be either effective or necessary. A three-second fuse would give the interceptor barely time to escape the fury of the blast it had directed. As the torpedoes left their tubes Sharrat fed power to the engines and darted away.

"Nothing." Fahey sounded baffled. "Those torps didn't detonate."

"Lieutenant!" Walcott called from the engine room. "Something's draining the power. Our screen's down!"

"Concentrate on maintaining the drive!" Sharrat accepted the need to escape. With a failing engine, torpedoes which didn't explode, he was helpless and knew it. "Fahey, use the guns, give that thing all you've got!!"

Self-propelled missiles which hurtled from the muzzles to send their charges of compressed destruction into the range glow. The stream of torpedoes, each as ineffective as the others. A rain of interceptor fragments, each capable of ripping through the hull of a normal vessel—none of which seemed to have the slightest effect on the thing which had appeared from nowhere.

The thing which gained on them even as Sharrat watched. Orange threads which extended to embrace the ship, to encompass it with a lambent haze. A glow of light which penetrated the very hull so that he seemed to be standing and looking through an orange tinted mist.

A mist in which, incredibly, both Fahey and Walcott were before him, apparently moved through solid metal itself.

And, with the mist, came voices.

"And these, brother?"

"More care, sister. We were hasty. These things are so delicate and yet so finely made. A welcome find, you agree?"

"At least we are not alone."

"As you feared. But the gamble was won and we live again. And now let us investigate a little. This one will do."

Walcott changed. He writhed and then was suddenly like a glove which has been turned inside out, a mess of steaming organs hanging nakedly visible, blood gushing like a crimson fountain, the stark white of bone wreathed with the blue-red of arteries and veins, the pulp of the brain a convoluted mass, the staring eyes like veined marbles.

A nightmare which shrieked once and then was mercifully silent.

"Too rough, brother. The thing is dead."

"But, dying, gave information. One other, then?"

"With care, brother."

"With care."

Fahey screamed. He reared onto the tips of his toes, a thicker haze of orange clustered around his head, vaporous fingers which thrust into his skull, giving him a grotesque halo as other fingers probed into his torso, his stomach.

A moment and then it was over, a limp sac falling where once had stood a man, a hollow bag of skin which collapsed on itself like a deflated, discarded balloon.

"Interesting, sister."

"Intriguing."

"And worthy of our attention. The possibilities are high, already I am amused. A challenge?"

"A wager, certainly, but the terms must be carefully arranged. Give me a moment for thought. Yes, I have it."

The concept of laughter, skirling notes in a careless tintinnabulation, cascades of ice chiming as they fell.

Numbed, immobile, Sharrat waited.

CHAPTER
TWO

Someone with a touch of imagination had decided that the Mare Serenis on Luna would make the ideal place to site a military hospital. The logic was sound; if names held any significance at all then the sick could only gain by being serene, but the biggest asset was the view the ambulatory cases could see through the transparent dome situated at one end of the complex.

Earth, Kennedy decided, could never be seen from a better place.

He stood before a window on the upper tier, neatly tall in civilian garments of silver grey edged with bronze, a contrast here where uniforms and functional whiteness was the rule. So much a contrast that a girl passing along the corridor halted to stare with frank appraisal at the broad shoulders sloping to the narrow waist, the hard planes and contours of his face, the firm line of the jaw and the mouth which, though now gentle, she sensed could become abruptly cruel.

A waste, she thought with the instant-opinion of youth. Such a man should be wearing a uniform and commanding a fleet. An impression heightened as he turned to look at her.

"Yes?"

"Nothing. I—that is—" She felt herself flush beneath the impact of his eyes and was annoyed at the unexpected reaction. He was a man and, as a nurse, she had seen many men.

"You wanted to know if you could help me. Is that it?"

"Yes." She was grateful for the lifeline. "I wondered if you were lost or something."

"No, just looking." Kennedy stepped aside to make room before the window. "Beautiful, isn't it."

A statement, not a question, and one which couldn't

be refuted. A globe of blended color, blue predominating, the swirls and contours of the ground hazed and blurred by cloud and distance, seas and continents adopting an unexpected configuration.

To a casual eye it looked a little like an artist's palette, to a more discerning it held the familiarity of a protoplasmic cell. A good analogy; from it men had grown to embrace the stars.

"Beautiful," she agreed and felt a strange reluctance that this moment would not last, that soon they would part perhaps never to meet again. "Could I help you?"

She couldn't, but it would have been unkind to have said so. Kennedy smiled and said, "I have an appointment with Doctor Durkan. If you could give me directions to her office?"

"I could take you."

"Thank you, but no." Kennedy softened the refusal. "You must be busy and I could find my way if you would give me the route. Room 4672, isn't it?"

"4675," she corrected, pleased to be of help. "Take the stair at the end of the corridor, turn right at the seventh level, you'll find it on your left."

She watched him go and then, sighing, hurried back to her ward.

Doctor Lydia Durkan was a woman who hid her age well. Taller than most she had a strongly boned face and deepset eyes of a luminous grey. Her mouth was wide, the lower lip full, her jaw expressing determination. She rose as Kennedy entered her office, the hand she extended broad, the fingers spatulate.

"Cap! It's good to see you again!"

"Lydia!" He felt the strength of her grip. "You don't look a day older than the last time we met and that was—what? Three years ago?"

"Four." Her eyes studied him, no longer young and far from impressionable, she had long since learned that appearances could be deceptive. Here was no idle dilletante who took care of his body but ignored stringent duty. "You're looking well, Cap. Any fresh scars?"

"A few."

"An occupational hazard to be expected, but take care, Cap. I don't want you to be delivered here in a sack one day. Don't get me wrong, but you're one patient I never want to see again."

"I'll take care of it."

"Maybe." She didn't sound confident. "I've been hearing things, Cap. You're getting quite a reputation."

"As you are yourself, Lydia."

"Rumor," she said casually. "We both know how it can grow."

But not in the service to which they both belonged.

Kennedy said, "The *Mordain* is over at the yards. The others will be reporting for routine examination within the hour. Take it easy with Jarl, Lydia, he's a little sensitive."

"He's getting old," she said flatly. "Just as I am, but he won't admit it. Well, maybe I can do something to help, but we haven't yet learned to perform miracles to order." She gestured to a couch set beside a diagnostic machine. "All right, Cap, let's get on with it. Strip and settle, you know the drill. I want a full and complete check on your physical condition."

"And?"

"Nothing more for now. Just get off those clothes and let me get to work."

Silently he obeyed, in this place and at this time the woman was in command. The electrodes held to his skin by adhesive pads made little sucking noises as they were finally removed. The vials of blood and other fluids collected as specimens vanished into the maw of a complex analyzer.

As he dressed, Kennedy said, quietly, "How's your special patient?"

"Waiting." A shadow touched her face. "If you can call it that. Waiting for someone to come along with skill enough to help. Waiting to die."

"We are all waiting to die," said Kennedy gently. "And you shouldn't blame yourself."

"Was I?"

The question held its own answer. A surgeon, a psychiatrist with degrees from the Newark University and the Rostov Foundation, the author of a dozen books and co-inventor of the Zirane-Durkan Technique, Lydia had betrayed her own feeling of inadequacy.

She added, savagely, "A lifetime of learning, Cap. A child prodigy—the one voted as the person most likely to succeed, and now I feel as if I know nothing. I'm helpless, damn it, and I don't like the feeling. And, what's more, I'm afraid."

A fear shared by Elias Weyburn.

He sat in a small office down on the lowest level, a place painted a soothing green with a facsimile window showing a view of rolling sward dotted with the bright blooms of summer flowers. He was a big man, the face sagging, the jowls heavy, the flesh graven with deeply impressed lines. His nose was beaked, his eyes pouched and, sitting at a desk, he gave the impression of a brooding eagle. A tired eagle, his shoulders rounded with the invisible weight of worlds.

A weight the Director of Terran Control knew, he would one day no longer be able to support.

Without preamble he said, "A bad one, Cap. A glowing ball of orange appeared from nowhere—did things— then vanished. That's all the real evidence we have."

Kennedy said, "There has to be more."

"There is." Weyburn was grim. "Film, records, a mess of data. We were lucky in a way—if you can call it luck—or perhaps we learned just what we were intended to discover. I couldn't tell you much over the radio for reasons you'll soon understand. And I don't want to tell you too much now—I want your unbiased opinion. But this I will say. It scares me, Cap. It scares me to hell."

An admission which augmented the taint of fear which Kennedy had sensed when he entered the office. A subtle something which emanated from Weyburn and which was in direct opposition to his nature. Concern, yes, and a healthy apprehension born of the awareness of impending danger, these were natural.

But the touch of naked terror which edged his voice and altered his scent—this was something new.

Kennedy said, slowly, "Elias—"

"Yes, Cap," Weyburn interrupted. "The thing we've always known might happen. The one thing we could never guard against—I think it's here."

Space was tremendous, a void filled with a multitude of stars, suns around which circled worlds, worlds on which diverse races had sprung into being. Races which had followed a pattern of evolution for reasons of which no one could be certain. A pattern of survival, perhaps, the common impress of the genetic code which dictated, within wide boundaries, the path intelligence should take. Humanoid structures with common affiliations; men who had sprung from avian ancestors, reptilian, the lepidoptera, the felines, the creatures who lurked in nighted seas. Aliens who lived beneath diverse suns and held customs and usages aligned to a spectrum of different cultures and societies and yet all, in a way, understandable.

Men who had learned to fight in order to survive. Races who knew the spur of ambition, the corrosive effects of envy and greed, the stirring of martial prowess. Young races eager to grab hold of empires and set their seed on a scatter of worlds, others old, content to dream of past glories.

Creatures with whom Weyburn could deal, using his hidden power to quash the fires of incipient war, moving in when diplomacy had failed and armed might threatened to spread atomic destruction among peaceful worlds.

Weyburn who sat like a spider at the center of a web, directing his agents, the Free Acting Terran Envoys, dedicated men of whom Kennedy was the foremost.

Men who would work in the dark, bribing, manipulating, killing if the need arose. The agents of FATE, each their own judge, jury and executioner. The hidden claws of the tiger which was Earth.

But, in the vastness of space, in the empty dark of unknown regions, could lurk other forms of life. Entities which had not followed a normal pattern of evolution. Creatures of incredible power against whom the race of man would be as ants to a sweeping fire.

And, one day, they could make contact.

Kennedy said, "Proof, Elias? Have we proof?"

Weyburn rose. Hitting a switch he said, "Lydia? Have you finished with Jarl yet? You have? Good. Bring him into the briefing room."

To Kennedy he added, "I think he should be in on this. Jarl's got a fine mind and, damn it, Cap, we need all the help we can get."

The briefing room was a long, narrow chamber, fitted with a screen at one end, chairs ranked before it, a table set in a cleared space at the far end. A room in which surgeons could discuss unusual cases; one in which the running of the hospital could be conducted in case of need.

In such a room uniforms belonged, but the men wearing them did not. Kennedy glanced at them, spotting Jud Harbin, the Military Supremo of Terran Armed Forces. At his side Conrad Weit, Chief of Diplomacy. Commander Breson caught his eye and nodded, his face grim. A small, fussy man sat facing a litter of pappers; Enrico Kozslik, an electronic genius, head of Terran Military research. Three others, all heavy brass.

Kennedy turned as Lydia Durkan entered the room, Professor Jarl Luden at her side.

He was slightly built, his figure sparse, almost boyish. He wore gaudy clothing, a personal eccentricity which gave him an oddly flamboyant appearance. His face was lined, a mass of thick, grey hair sweeping back from a high forehead. His eyes were deepset, a vivid blue glowing with the light of intelligence. His lips were thin, downturned as if he had tasted something not to his liking.

As he dropped into a chair beside Kennedy he snapped, waspishly, "That woman! I am perfectly fit as I told her, but she insisted on treating me as if I were a laboratory specimen. Someone should tell her that a man needs to maintain both his dignity and pride."

"An examination, Jarl," soothed Kennedy. "We're all having one."

"And all this elaborate secrecy." Luden, unmollified, glowered at the assembly. "Another few days and we might have discovered something of real value on Vyath. That fragment bore the traces of the Zheltyana Seal and other fragments could have been excavated had we the time."

"Gentlemen!" Harbin's big hand slammed on the table. "And you, Madam." He nodded at the woman. "This is in the nature of a special inquiry. I don't intent to waste time on trivia, but just for the record—"

The screen flared to life as he hit a button.

It depicted an area of space glowing with stars, in the foreground a twisted mass of metal which had once been a ship.

"An interceptor—one of fifteen destroyed during the recent exercise conducted by Mobile Aid Laboratory and Construction Authority Number 7, Commander Breson in charge." Harbin's voice was flat, unemotional. "A full investigation has shown that no blame can be attached to Commander Breson. In fact he is commended for adaptability and adherence to duty. The introduction of a novel and entirely unexpected event did not prevent him from continuing the exercise in which he was engaged."

The image vanished to be replaced by another.

"The ball of orange luminescence which you see was recorded and transmitted by the observation scanner in the interceptor commanded by Lieutenant Edward Sharrat. As you will observe, offensive action was taken without apparent result. The two other units of the squad were totally destroyed. Sharrat's vessel, after a brief period of time, was also demolished—but first it relayed this information."

Kennedy heard the sharp intake of breath from those watching the shambles.

As the screen went dark Harbin said, "And that is really all we know. All else is and must be surmise. Kozslik!"

The fussy man cleared his throat.

"From examination of the wrecked vessels I have determined that no apparent armament was used. The best analogy I can make is that of a man folding and tearing a tin can. The forces involved would leave no trace other than a slight crystallization of the metal itself."

Luden said sharply, "Was any such crystallization found?"

"No."

"Which means there was no flexing. The forces applied were in one direction only. Time?"

"The destruction was apparently instantaneous," said Kozslik. He picked up one of his papers. "Instantaneous and wide spread. The interceptors involved occupied various positions around the mother ship. The space between them averaged to a quarter light-year. I think it safe to assume that the powers controlling the destructive force could just as easily demolish the mother ship itself as the scattered interceptors."

"An unwarranted conclusion," said Luden acidly. "There could be limiting factors of which we are as yet unaware. The mass of an interceptor is minute compared to that of the main vessel."

"True," admitted Kozslik. "Yet the wide-spread distribution gives rise to the possibility that sheer mass need not be a limiting factor. Taking the total—"

"Forget it!" Weyburn's voice cracked from where he sat at the table. "All this nitpicking can wait. Jud, let's get to the heart of the matter. First, what do we have? Something alien suddenly appears in space, does things to some members of a crew then knocks hell out of a bunch of interceptors. Atomics couldn't hurt it and neither could anything else we could throw its way. Conclusion?"

"The utilization of a new form of energy," said Luden at once. "Both for defensive and offensive purposes."

"And?"

"A test," said Lydia Burkan. "Those men—I've done vivisections myself."

"So?"

"Whoever or whatever was in that orange light was curious," said Kennedy. "They'd bumped into something strange and made an investigation. They could have waited but didn't. That shows they are either impatient or operate on a different time framework from ours." He added slowly, "It also shows they have mastery of techniques far superior to our own."

"Agreed!" Weyburn glowered around the table. "As I see it we're facing trouble. We can't hide from it by worrying about trivia—not at the moment. Conrad!"

The Head of Diplomacy drew in his breath.

"This sounds crazy, but the facts can't be denied. Lieutenant Edward Sharrat appeared in five places at the same time; in the stadium on Kronchot, in the forum of Enderis, at the spacefield on Huleth, in the gymnasium on Isa and in the Senate on Earth. In each place he gave the same message."

"Wait!" Luden leaned forward a little over the table. "When you say at the same time do you mean that literally?"

"I do." Weit anticipated the next question. "I've treble-checked. Recordings were made at three of the places and we have witnesses to the rest. There could possibly be an error of a few seconds, a minute at the most, but that would be because of human incapability. The mechanical sources leave no doubt."

"And the time?" Luden was insistent. "Did he appear before or after the destruction of the interceptors?"

"Before." Weit checked his notes. "He appeared and vanished. The interceptors were destroyed then."

"Vanished?"

"To here," said Lydia Durkan. "Lieutenant Edward Sharrat appeared in the hospital as naked as the day he was born. He is still here." She added somberly, "What is left of him."

He was quite mad.

He appeared dressed in a loose smock of pale green, the attendants at his side gentle as they guided him toward the end of the table, supporting him as he stood, swaying, unable even to maintain his balance. His face was blank as a virgin sheet of paper, all the tiny details etched by time and experience washed away, the muscles lax, without volition.

It was impossible for him to smile, to even focus his eyes.

He was no longer a man.

"We've taught him to walk," said Lydia Durkan bitterly. "He's about as capable at it as a two-year old; worse. It's a matter of falling and hoping that the involuntary system operates to maintain stability. Sometimes he manages a dozen steps, at others only two. Mostly he just lies and stares at nothing—only when we don't close his eyes to maintain liquidity of the eyeballs."

One of the attendants, as if at a command, lowered each lid of the blankly staring eyes.

"He can't hear," continued the doctor. "Or if he can I have no way of telling. I think that the sounds are no longer transmitted to the relevant portions of the brain. Visual images too, touch, taste, smell—all five senses inoperative."

Kennedy said, "Brain damage?"

"Not that I can determine." Lydia Durkan's voice reflected her sense of helplessness. "That's the trouble, I can't be sure of anything. I can only guess."

"And?"

"They took him," she said bitterly. "They—whoever was responsible. They took him and they changed him. His brain has been altered on a neurone-level so that he isn't a man anymore. He's just a machine. Something to carry a message." Her voice rose a little. "Don't you understand? They wanted a messenger and they made one. They took this poor devil and turned him into a living facsimile of a recorder."

Kennedy said harshly, "And the message?"

"A challenge. A game. We win and they let us alone. We lose and—" Her hand lifted, gestured toward the roof, the area above, the transparency of the dome, the ball of Earth "—they wipe us out. They take Earth and they eliminate it and everything on it. A game, Cap! They call it a game!"

CHAPTER
THREE

They called themselves the Sukhi—if they had mouths with which to form words or had any need of a label at all. But labels are necessary when dealing with primitive beings and also, perhaps it was an indulgence to the need of personal identification. The ego which can only be expressed as something unique.

Or, again, it could have been only a part of the game they were playing.

The diversion which they intended to give them a moment of pleasure.

Kennedy touched the switch of the recorder and listened to the voice which had once belonged to a man. An odd voice, with subtle overtones, a hint of mirth, a lighthearted casualness as if nothing done or said could have the least importance.

". . . as the Sukhi. What and who we are and from where we came need not concern you, but you may think of us as two, as male and female, Balik and Avura, such small details will amuse you as the game will amuse us. A simple game based on the basic elements of life itself and incorporating a jest of a delicate nature. Only the strong deserve to survive; therefore prove your worth or vanish from the face of the cosmos. But how? The wager must be carefully balanced and so. . . ."

The voice died as Kennedy threw the switch. He had heard it for too long, would hear it again, but for now he had heard enough.

"Words," said Weyburn. Brandy stood on a small table beneath the facsimile window in the small office and he crossed to it, poured, swallowed a generous measure at a gulp. "Well, Cap, you've heard. You know as much as I do, as much as they do." His head jerked toward the briefing room, the men it contained. "What do you think?"

Kennedy said, "The details. They don't add up somehow. The logic seems all wrong. We aren't meeting their challenge at all. They want us to prove that we are the best on our own terms."

"At the Galactiad." Weyburn helped himself to more brandy, needing the spirit for fuel, to fire the wasted energies of his body. For days now, Kennedy guessed, he had been denying himself rest, operating with the aid of drugs to combat the threat against Earth. "Sharrat," he said. "He was a sports buff and would have known all about the Galactiad. It's obvious they took everything they wanted to know from his mind. Wiped it clean then sent him out with that damned message."

A message he had forgotten now. Kennedy remembered how he had looked as they had guided him away. An empty shell, his purpose served, now a useless discard. A thing over which the medics would labor, trying, hoping to learn, to rekindle what had once been. Trying and failing as they would have to fail.

"Five places," said Kennedy. "And then here. Why here?" He knew the answer. "He didn't know about Terran Control, but every spaceman knows about Serenis."

"Right on our doorstep," said Weyburn grimly. "The Senate and then here. If it was just that I wouldn't be so worried, but how the hell can we hope to keep this quiet? Earth wins the Galactiad or Earth is destroyed. Even if the Chambodians don't believe it they won't miss the chance. And there are others who would love to see us exterminated, the Haddrach of Holme, the Inchonians, the Sifurians—you name them and they'll be on the line cheering our defeat."

Glass shattered to fall like glistening rain and Weyburn looked at his hand, the thread of blood from the cut on his palm, the blood which dripped to join the ruined glass on the floor.

"Defeat," he said thickly. "Earth wiped out, all we've worked for, suffered, gone through—for this!"

A game to amuse bored aliens and Weyburn wasn't talking in personal terms. He was thinking of the long millennia during which mankind had struggled from the mud, to fight through blood and pain, to reach the stars and to leave behind them a virtual paradise. The near-Utopia which Earth had become.

"We've got to win, Cap." Weyburn shook his hand then wrapped his handkerchief around the wound. "We've got to play this game as the Sukhi dictate— we've no choice. They've shown us their power—those ships were destroyed so that we would know they could do what they promised if we didn't play along. Moving Sharrat about, that was another demonstration. Harbin is beating his head against a wall when he talks of massing out defenses and he knows it. Weit can't do a damned thing—friends vanish when you're in trouble. It's up to us, Cap."

As, in the final essence, it was always up to them, thought Weyburn bleakly. When diplomacy failed and armed might was useless what else was left but a dagger in the dark?

Kennedy said, "So we've got to win the Galactiad. What are our chances?"

"Not good enough." Weyburn glanced at the bottle then decided against another drink. He still had a long way to go before he could call it a day. "If we had a hundred percent top performers, they still wouldn't be good enough. This is one game we daren't lose, Cap, and we can't afford to take chances. A contender could fall sick, tear a muscle, anything. And there'll be a lot around to help him do it. They've got to be stopped and so has anyone who has a winning edge. You don't need me to spell it out for you."

"No," said Kennedy dryly. "You don't."

"Sport has nothing to do with this, Cap. It's a battle for survival. The main trouble is the time factor. All contenders are booked in together with trainers, coaches and handlers, and it's too late to arrange an exchange or to alter the standing. I've got an expert on the games who will give you a rundown on the contenders, their likelihood of winning, the usual stuff. You can study it on the way."

Weyburn crossed to the door leading to the briefing room, cracked it, listened.

"They're still at it," he said. "Talking, but there's not much else they can do. Anyway it gives Jarl a chance to absorb the details. I'll have him at the *Mordain* in an hour. You'd better check out with Lydia."

She was back in her office studying a sheet of finely printed detail, vials lying before her, a photograph of a smiling girl holding a baby on her desk. Something Kennedy had never seen before.

"A relative?"

"My young sister." She glanced at it. "She married a military technician based at the Dallas Port. That baby is seven now and the brightest girl in her class. They say she takes after me." One hand lifted to touch the line of her jaw. "I hope they are just trying to be kind."

"They don't have to be that, Lydia."

"No," she admitted. "They don't have to be—but it helps if they are."

She had deliberately mistaken his meaning and he wondered if there was more to the association than what he knew. Wondered too why she had chosen to display the photograph, but that question was easily answered.

"They aren't going to die, Lydia."

"We all die, Cap."

He said, "You've been too close to Sharrat. What you've seen has worried you sick. You're thinking of your sister and her child, what they would be like if the Sukhi carried out their threat. Don't worry, Lydia, in this crazy game they've set up they aren't going to win."

"And how will you stop them?" she said bitterly. "With atomics? Guns? Poison? Can you even begin to guess at the power they must have? What they did to that officer—I've spent my life studying the mind and I don't know what was done. Erasure, yes and a strong impression similar to a post-hypnotic command, but what else? The disorientation is total. The actual neurone manipulation has—"

"I know," he said curtly. "You told us."

"Did I?" She lifted her hands to her eyes and pressed the heels of the palms into their sockets. Lowering them she said, "I'm tired, I guess, and forgetful. How do you take a normal, living brain and transform it into a machine? One with a built-in destruct mechanism. That's what's wrong with him, Cap. He's done his job and now he has no reason to continue to exist. If you were me how would you treat him?"

"With a Dione!" Kennedy was deliberately cold. "I'd put a blast through his skull and give him peace. Him and you and everyone who has to see him and take care of him. And, if you don't like the idea of a gun, then give him a drop of poison."

"You'd do it," she said. "I can't. Call it a weakness if you like, but while he lives I'll keep trying."

"I know." He was suddenly gentle. "I guess that's what makes you the kind of person you are. The kind of doctor young students admire. There's nothing wrong with you, Lydia. You've just got a strong dose of humanity."

"As you have, Cap." Her eyes met his own, the luminous grey searching, direct. "That's why you do what you do, are what you are. Have you never thought about giving it all up, just moving on and on, looking for something new?"

"At times, yes."

"I'd have called you a liar had you said different. Why do you carry on?"

Casually he said, "Why not? It's a job."

"Which you don't need."

"Excitement, then."

"Which you could do without. There's nothing amusing in risking your neck every time you go to clear up a mess."

"True, but someone has to clear away the garbage."

"Yes," she admitted, "And it's always the best who

are willing to do it. You, Elias—" She broke off, shaking her head as if annoyed at herself for yielding to sentiment. And yet, in the intimacy which they shared, the moment of closeness in which barriers were down and secrets could be spoken, it was hard not to say more.

"Elias—"

"Is a slave-driver," said Kennedy quickly. "A hard, tough, dedicated man."

Too hard and too dedicated, perhaps, his position gained at too high a price. The cost of loneliness, the bleak isolation of command. Of never being able to share his doubts and worries, the iron resolve which made him what he was denying him the normal pleasures of a wife and family. To him Earth was his first and only love. To those that loved him a mistress they could never hope to equal.

As Lydia, perhaps, had once hoped. As she could still hope—but Kennedy was determined to spare her the regret of exposing her inner hurt.

"He sent me to you," he said. "Something about checking out. Did you find anything wrong?"

For a second she sat as if frozen and then, with a brief shake of the head, said, "No, Cap. You're a perfect specimen of a Terran male. However, as a doctor, I would advise all my nurses to stay well clear of you. We still haven't found a cure for a broken heart."

The moment had passed, irony raising a defense, their relationship now back on its normal level. Yet things were not quite as they had been. Each knew a little more about the other and, knowing, felt less alone.

"And Jarl?"

"A deception. Old he might be but he's as hard as a barrel of nails. Penza—well it would take a steam hammer to hurt him, and Veem's made of rubber. You all check out as fit for arduous duty."

"Which wasn't what you wanted to find out," Kennedy said shrewdly. "Just what did Elias want you to do?"

"Help." Again her eyes met his. "Each to their own, Cap, and we do what we can. I had to check to determine tolerance levels and metabolic function." She gestured at the vials. "I can't turn you into a superman, Cap, but I can give you a little help against men who've trained to do a single thing for the majority of their lives. You and Jarl—the others don't come into it."

"Drugs?"

"Something to raise the pain level. I know it's high but we can make it higher. Something else to banish fatigue. And something to eliminate the safety-factor on muscular exertion. You can do it by use of the Clume Discipline, I know, but this is faster. And all are undetectable by the tests normally used at the Galactiad."

He said, "And poison?"

"That too. It won't kill but give it to an athlete and he won't be at the top of his form. There's an antidote geared to your particular metabolism—also undetectable." She added, a little bitterly, "They used to call it sport."

"They did," he agreed. "Back in the old days before planetary pride took over. Now the Galactiad is more like a war. And it's one we've got to win."

"You'll win it, Cap. You've got to!"

She stood for a long moment after he had gone, staring blindly at the photograph, the smiling girl and the babe now grown. A new life nurtured in a womb—and experience she had never known and now would never know.

Once there had been a chance, but dedication was a harsh taskmaster and work, endless work, had provided an anodyne. It would be ironic if all that work had been wasted.

Leaving the office she went down the passage to the door of the small room painted green. The facsimile window was bright with color, light which showed the broken glass, the telltale stains of blood. Blood which had dripped to form a trail which led to the stairs, to the upper tier, to the figure standing limned in Earthlight, his head thrown back, the shoulders now no longer bowed.

Weyburn looking at his love.

He didn't turn as she halted beside him but his hand reached out to grip her own, to hold it tight. And it was enough.

To each their own.

And, as Kennedy had said, someone had to clear up the garbage.

CHAPTER
FOUR

In the control room of the *Mordain* Chemile leaned back in the big chair and listened to the soft susurration of Heddish drums coming from a recorder. With the controls on automatic his presence was unnecessary, yet his eyes constantly drifted over the monitors and instruments on the consol. A habit, should anything threaten, the screens would divert or dissipate the danger, the ship itself moving to avoid anything too large to handle otherwise.

It was a chance to sit and relax, to dream of the departed glories of his ancient race. Glories which had little basis in fact, but which he liked to air from time to time. Especially when invited to address one of the groups of women who formed cultural clubs on Earth and other worlds. Plump matrons, usually bored, who hung on his every word and felt a vicarious thrill at his recounting of dire perils.

But relaxing was for periods of inactivity. Now the *Mordain* was heading at top speed toward Regak—the site of the Galactiad.

"Veem." Saratov entered the control room. "I've made coffee."

The engineer was a creature from Earth's ancient mythology, a trogdolite of legend. Almost as wide as he was tall, the shaven ball of his skull fell to a thick neck which blended into massive shoulders. Arms, thighs and torso completed the resemblance to a living machine made of toughened bone and muscle. The product of a high-gravity world, he had, while wearing his usual loose robes, often been mistaken for a normal man grown obscenely fat. A mistake several had made to their cost.

Chemile took the coffee, sipped, said, "You're improving, Penza. This is almost drinkable."

Saratov didn't rise to the bait. He had other things on his mind than to indulge in the usual banter which gave outsiders the impression that the friends were deadly rivals.

Chemile sensed it and lapsed into silence. He was tall, slender, his eyes tiny jewels set in the smooth ovoid of his face. His ears were like shells set against his skull, peaked, delicate. His skin was covered with minute flecks of photosensitive tissue which gave him the ability to adopt the coloration of any background against which he stood. A defensive measure developed on the savage world on which he had been born, a chameleon-like protection against local predators which depended on sight, not scent to track their prey.

"We didn't stay long enough on Luna," said Saratov. "I wanted to recheck the engines, but there wasn't time."

"There's nothing wrong with the engines."

"I like to be sure."

Chemile shrugged, knowing that to the giant anything less than perfection was unacceptable as far as the *Mordain* was concerned. He said, "How about taking some coffee to Cap and Jarl?"

They were in the laboratory, sitting hunched over a mass of papers, details of games and contenders. Kennedy accepted the coffee, leaning back, easing the strain from neck and shoulders. Luden sipped, swallowed, set down the cup.

Chemile said, "How's it going, Jarl?"

"Slowly." Luden thinned his lips as he studied the graphs he had made. "The difficulty in dealing with human elements is the tremendously wide spectrum of variables, which makes any prediction open to doubt. A contender may be at the top of his form one day, the next a bad dream, a touch of indigestion, even a mood could entirely alter his performance."

"So you can't isolate the winners," said Saratov.

"No one can, Penza." Luden was sharp. "Gamblers since the dawn of time have been trying to do exactly that and failing with unending consistency. The best we can do is to isolate areas of maximum probability and then do our best to ensure that favorable results are obtained."

"So we fix the events." The giant shrugged. "Simple."

Kennedy said dryly, "Have you ever been to a Galactiad, Penza? No? I thought not. It isn't as simple as you think."

"How come?"

"Contenders are selected on a basis of elimination," explained Luden patiently. Unconsciously his tone adopted the attributes of a lecturer addressing a class of students. "These preliminary bouts are held on the various competing worlds or groups of worlds. Obviously there isn't room or facilities for every known world to enter its own team. Earth, for example, has a team composed of residents or members of affiliated planets which fall within rigid specifications as regards to gravity etc. You, for example, as a native of Droom, would not be allowed to join the Terran team."

"A pity. I could take care of weight-lifting, for example."

"Which is the reason for the restrictions," Luden pointed out. "Otherwise the entire Galactiad would become a farce. However, to continue, the final selections are entered, registered, and placed in the facilities provided on Regak. Here is the first problem. As rivalry is intense, all contenders are heavily guarded and the rules closely followed. Substitutions are allowed but only under stringent precautions. A security blanket isolates the contenders and unauthorized visits are not permitted. The possibility of cheating is always present, naturally, as is actual physical harm to the contenders. Dangers of which the local authorities are well aware. As Regak depends on the revenue of the games to form the major portion of its income their concern is natural."

"What you're saying, Jarl, is that we just can't walk in and get to work. Right?"

"The initial problem in a nutshell, Penza."

And one to be expected. Saratov watched as Luden

turned to the computer and sent his fingers dancing over the keys, using the machine to do in seconds what would take an unaided brain weeks.

Less patient, Chemile said, "So what can we do about it?"

"We must isolate all relevant factors and, on a basis of elimination, use the best means we have to achieve the desired result." Luden explained as he worked. "The Chambodians, for example, have a team which includes a runner of remarkable prowess. On the basis of available information the closest threat to his winning is a Killurian from the Haddrach of Holme. Our own entrant appears to stand little chance, but if the Chambodian entry was to be eliminated and something should happen to the Killurian, the prospect would look brighter."

Saratov said bleakly, "Just how many contenders do we have to fix? How many events can we be sure of winning?"

"All and none, Penza."

The only correct answer born of Luden's habit of being exactly precise. In no athletic contest could certainty of winning be guaranteed unless all opposition was removed—in which case there would be no competition and no essential first place gained.

"This could have been done in a different way," rumbled the giant. "Harbin could have sent in a MALACA and taken over the games. That way we'd be sure of winning."

The simple, enticing solution, but one impossible to achieve, as Saratov knew. To have done it would have been to start an interstellar war; an excuse for the Chambodians and others to flock to the defense of Regak, to have filled space with ravening destruction.

A fact which did not eliminate the wish—but there was no certainty that the mysterious Sukhi would have accepted the result so gained.

As Luden's hands fell from the computer, Kennedy said, "Did you learn anything new at the briefing, Jarl?"

"No, we simply went over the same ground. Kozslik

is baffled though I must admit I can find no fault with his manner of conducting the investigation. Many of his conclusions are valid despite the lack of substantiating proof. It is obvious that the aliens are of a totally unfamiliar nature and I am intrigued at the multiple appearance of Sharrat. A demonstration of power, of course, but it would be interesting to determine how it was done." Luden's voice held the yearning of the scientist dedicated to the pursuit of knowledge.

Saratov said, "Surely it must have been done by actual duplication, Jarl. The time element precludes the possibility of instantaneous transmission. An object can only be in one place at one time."

"As far as we know," corrected Luden. "It would be a mistake to place accepted limitations on the science of the aliens. And the use of the term instantaneous transmission tends to hide the fact that, logically, there can be no such thing. An object is either here or somewhere else. For it to be moved a fraction of time, no matter how small, has to be involved. For us it could be indiscernible—to others not."

"You suspect a manipulation of the temporal flow?" Kennedy touched one of the papers, a report, and studied it again. "From the exercise area, Sharrat was sent to one of five places—it doesn't matter which. He stayed long enough to give his message and to repeat it three times. A period of six minutes. A half hour in all before he appeared at Serenis. If he had been duplicated the five surrogates could have been adjusted to be self-eliminating, but in that case why bother to send him to Luna at all?"

"Another demonstration," said Chemile. "Or they wanted to make quite sure we understood the terms of the challenge."

"Or there was only the one man and they sent him around." Saratov scowled, thinking. "If so then they must have moved him back in time in order to give the impression of duplication. Each time he vanished he was moved back and sent somewhere else."

"That is a possibility, Penza," said Kennedy. "But there is another."

Luden said, shrewdly, "Facsimile projection?"

"It fits."

Saratov said, blankly, "Fits what, Cap? A man can't be at several places at the same time."

"If he was a man." Kennedy leaned back his eyes narrowed with speculation. "Suppose we managed to fashion an electronic ghost image of the *Mordain*? On an enemy screen it would appear as an actual ship, right?"

"If they relied solely on simple electronic monitoring," agreed the giant. "But no ship would do that. They'd use the Larvic-Shaw and visual aids and other things. A ghost would be spotted for what it was."

"Only if the watching ship had the equipment with which to do it," said Chemile, understanding. "And a man is limited to the scope of his senses. Do you think those appearances were just tri-dimensional projections, Cap?"

"I hope so, Veem."

"Hope?"

"I don't like the alternative," said Kennedy grimly. "The possibility that, in some way, they managed to project an actual portion of themselves. If they did, it means they could be anywhere at any time and in any shape they chose to adopt."

"Like the Mimics of Dephene," said Saratov. "Their natural ability to alter shape coupled with the power of instantaneous transmission. All right, Jarl, maybe it is a misleading term, but we're stuck with it."

"You said a portion of themselves, Cap," said Chemile. "How—"

"Like this." Kennedy slapped his hand on the table. Spreading the fingers he said, "Think of an ant watching that hand. What does it see? A finger—I change it to a thumb, a fist, a palm. Different shapes and each a part of myself. Would the ant know that? Could it guess that I only used a portion of my being? And remember the message, the fact that two beings were mentioned. My guess is that they were putting complicated relationships into terms we could understand."

"Aping humanity," said Luden. "Let us hope they manage to restrain their curiosity."

"Yes," said Kennedy grimly. "We've got a hard enough job ahead of us as it is without those damned aliens taking an active, personal interest. Well, if they do there's nothing to prevent them. Let's get on with the details, Jarl. Just how many events can we be reasonably certain of winning?"

The coffee grew cold, more, provided at regular intervals, remaining barely touched. As the *Mordain* hurtled through space at a velocity which made the speed of light a mere crawl facts and items were collated, set aside, others manipulated, the computer kept busy as, slowly, the essential information was isolated.

"We are fortunate in that the trophy goes to the team with the highest aggregate of points," said Luden. He looked tired, his eyes sore, the lines on his face accentuated by his pallor. "Five for the actual winner and graded down to one for the competitor taking fourth place. The winner gets an extra bonus point."

"Five, three, two, one," said Kennedy. "Technically a team could win the trophy without ever having actually won an event."

"Unlikely, but true," agreed Luden. "Naturally individual winners receive an award, but we are not concerned with that. The system, of course, has been designed to both stimulate competition and to maintain a high pitch of interest. Not until the last event has taken place can the actual winner of the trophy be determined. Now, according to our findings, the teams of Oyte, Muhl, Vaney, Guisa, and Cho'loctacol each hold a dangerous factor of undeterminable magnitude. Tayoy is also a problem."

"One which will have to wait." Kennedy studied the list. Like Luden he was tired, fatigue dragging at his eyes and fogging his brain. Drugs would provide an anodyne, but he resisted the temptation. There would be little point in using them now and there were good reasons why he should not. "We're lucky that Chambodia has no team—those damned vultures don't go in for competitive sports, but we can be certain they will be taking an active interest. Well, that's something else which will have to wait. Let's see if we can do something to even things out."

Kennedy contacted Terran Control. To the girl who appeared on the screen, the beauty of her face carried across the void by the magic of hybeam radio, he said, "Get me a direct link to Conrad Weit."

"I think he's in conference, Cap."

"Then get him out of it. This is urgent. Move!"

Weit looked haggard. His normally bland features reflected the strain of the events which had thrown him from his course of delicate maneuvering, the battles he fought using words as weapons. A man who appeared softer than he was, a carefully cultivated pose which served as a mask to hide his determination, an iron resolve no less than Kennedy's own though expressed in different ways.

The ways of men who had learned to lie, to talk without words, to recognize a message in a subtle turn of phrase, an inflection, the lift of an eyebrow. To haggle and bargain and always to seek an advantage. The ways of the market despite the resounding titles and expensive clothes, the glitter and luxury of embassies and palaces.

Kennedy could understand it, recognize its value, but tedious diplomacy was not for him. A man of action, he had little patience and less liking for the world to which Conrad Weit belonged.

"Cap?"

"Take down this list," said Kennedy, and read out the names. "Got them?"

"Yes, but if you're thinking of trying to buy them off, forget it. I've been through that."

"Then go through it again," snapped Kennedy. "Damn it, Conrad, we must be owed some favors. This is the time to claim them."

"Do you think I haven't tried?" Weit was bitter. "The vultures are gathering for the feast. I've had a dozen hints and warnings. Treaties which should have been signed and sealed by now are still pending. Trade missions which regret that they cannot meet their schedules, others abruptly cancelled. Three planets are already hinting of seceding from the Terran Sphere. And it'll get worse, Cap. Every vessel leaving Earth is packed with visitors on the run." He added grimly, "And not only visitors."

The rich, the idle, the dilettantes, those with a high regard for their skins, others who had yielded to panic.

Rats deserting a sinking ship.

They were unimportant, a thin scum which could never be wholly eliminated from any culture.

"Forget them," said Kennedy. "Now how about that list? Oyte should play along and, as I remember, Cho'loctacol owes us something. Work on them and the others. We've got to get some of those teams withdrawn. I don't care how you do it or what you have to promise, it has to be done."

"I've tried—"

"Try again and don't be afraid of using pressure. If Earth goes down we have nothing to lose."

A fact Weit had been reluctant to accept. A victim of his profession, he had been too delicate, and yet within the man there was iron. Some of it showed in his eyes, the set of his mouth, the abrupt jutting of his jaw.

"You're right, Cap, this is no time for kid gloves. I'll start leaning, but there's opposition. The Haddrach of Holme, the Chambodians—"

"Will be working in the opposite direction," agreed Kennedy. "They don't have to win—all they need to do is to stop us getting the trophy. Get with it, Conrad and don't pull your punches!"

What could be done he would do, giving away concessions, making veiled threats, using the old, familiar and trusted means of hidden bribery, manipulating political futures and presenting the bill for past favors.

Bills accompanied with a grim alternative if they weren't paid.

Even if Earth should be destroyed the MALACAs would remain and false friends would be remembered.

The rest would be done on Regak.

CHAPTER
FIVE

It was a lonely world; a single planet circling the swollen ball of a dying sun, the orb mottled and stained with penumbra and flocculi so that to a casual glance it held the appearance of a senile and sneering old man.

Like the sun, the planet was old, the mountains worn, the seas lying like stagnant pools in almost empty beds, shores ringed with encrusted weed, the surface of the residual oceans broken from time to time by monstrous shapes, crustaceans and fish which, mutating, had survived.

The Regakians followed the pattern of their world.

Tall, slim, with faces from which all emotion had eroded away, odd humps rising between their shoulders, their eyes enormous in the confines of their skulls. Once they had known the bitter fury of internecine war—the ruins of blasted cities remained as a mute testimony to the insanity which once had ruled—now they and their world were dedicated to the games which took place every five years. The Galactiad which drew contenders and spectators from a host of worlds.

Both were tolerated for the money they brought with them.

And, with them, came the parasites.

Kennedy saw them as he led the way from the cluttered field, the *Mordain* safely locked and resting to one side. A gaggle of pimps, touts, harlots, gamblers, entrepreneurs, men who sold dainties from mobile stands, girls who told fortunes, women who called and screamed and laughed in a near-hysteria. The usual conglomeration to be found on any world where pickings were to be had and few counted the cost of their pleasures.

"Master! A wager! Ten decals will get you fifty if I fail to eat a Wenedian pie in less than five minutes!"

The man who spread arms wide before Kennedy wore silver and gold, tinsel stained with tarnish, the upper part of his face hidden beneath the mask of a bear. A fool, drunk of jesting, or perhaps a man desperate with hunger, willing to risk the fate of a welcher for the sake of the food he would gulp.

Kennedy shook his head.

"A gift then! A token! A single decal and I will pray your team to victory!"

Saratov rumbled, "Why not, Cap? We could do with the help."

He was half-joking but Kennedy was serious as again he shook his head. The coin was nothing—the man would be satisfied with a minim, but once thrown it would attract a crowd of eager suppliants who had scented an easy mark.

"You! Be off! You bother our guests!"

The guard, and during the Galactiad every male Regakian who was not involved with the games was a guard, gestured at the tarnished figure. He was armed, the butt of a Dione rising from the holster strapped around his narrow waist, but he made no move toward the weapon. Even if he used it the searing shaft of energy would burn air, not flesh. Only in extremes and when there was no other way to control a hostile demonstration or to halt a running killer, would fire burn its way into flesh and sinew.

To use a gun was an act of war—and Regak had had enough of war.

To Kennedy the guard said. "Our apologies for the incident, sir, but the man meant no harm. I suggest that, if such things incommode you or your party, you take one of the transports to your hotel. You have a hotel?"

"As yet, no."

"I see." The guard frowned, thinking, eager to be of help. "A bad time to make a late booking, sir, but if you have no objection to travel, the Etumish Tower is to be recommended. It lies to the south on the shore of the

Virbrent Pool. Or there is the Phlegarian Hotel, that lies to the north close to the ruins of Eccavack."

"How far?"

"An hour's flight to each."

Too far, time was too precious to waste and Kennedy had made other arrangements though he didn't say so. Guards, like all men, could be the bearers of information.

Casually he said, "We will look around. Should nothing else be available I shall remember your suggestions. In the meantime, for luck—" A coin changed hands. The customary offering, a tradition carefully advertised and a steady source of added income from superstitious gamblers.

"Thank you, sir." The guard was polite. "May good fortune attend you and your teams. Make way there!" He waved a path through the crowd. "Should you require transport, ground cars wait at the end of the avenue."

They were low, wide-bodied, small engined, each with an attendant driver and all brightly painted in a variety of colors.

Halting, Kennedy said, "Penza, take Veem and find a hotel, if you can, close to the stadium. Report to the Terran camp, I'll tell them to expect you. Jarl, we'll go straight there."

"Riding?"

"Walking."

Luden fell into step as Kennedy forged ahead. The streets was crowded, gay with bunting, the visitors and touts filling the air with raucous noise. A girl, young, soft flesh showing beneath a slitted gown, her face a psychedelic mask, caught Kennedy by the arm, her voice an inviting whisper.

"Like to play some interesting games, handsome? A full repertoire—and in the stadium of my bed you can't lose."

A Cissurian skilled in the exotic and erotic arts.

Smiling, Kennedy said, "No thank you—but I appreciate the offer."

"Then why refuse it?" Her eyes searched his face, his

body beneath the somber black edged with gold, civilian garments which did little to hide the lithe tautness of his figure. "For you a special rate. Good food, good wine and music if you want it. I can dance too and—well, why not yield to temptation."

As again he shook his head the girl turned to Luden.

"Nothing like old wine," she said boldly. "And the best tunes come from old fiddles. How about giving me an education, Pop?"

"Really!" Luden was stiff. "Madam, I assure you that your charms, attractive as they undoubtedly are, have little appeal for me. I suggest that you cease wasting your time."

"It's my time." Her hand rose to flick the mane of his hair. "But, for you, Pop, it's running out. Why not make the most of what's left? No? Well, change your mind and I'll be around here if you want me. Good luck at the games."

Smiling, she turned away to accost a plump man wearing silken green and scarlet, the glitter of gems at his fingers, a speculative gleam in his eye. The woman at his side, old, painted, closed her fingers firmly on his arm.

"No, Arald," she said. "Remember your promise." Then, to the girl, said spitefully, "Vanish, slut! Get lost before I tear out your eyes!"

"You old hag!"

"You harlot! You scum! How dare you flaunt yourself at my man!"

"Bitch!"

"Now, ladies," said the plump man weakly. "There's no need for this. Suse, we should be getting along. And you, my dear—"

"I'll see you here tonight," shouted the Cissurian. "When you've put mother to bed."

The shriek of rising argument faded as Kennedy walked on. The incident was nothing, a minor brawl soon forgotten. But, later, as the games progressed, there would be uglier episodes; men robbed and beaten, losers desperate for a fresh stake and willing to risk the watchful guards, gamblers who had plunged too deeply and eager to recoup their losses.

Then the guards would earn their pay.

Kennedy glanced at the sky. It was late, the sun a somber ball low over the peaked roofs to the west, patches of shadow holding ruby shimmers and seeming to paint the city with the color of blood. From a point somewhere ahead a rocket soared upwards to explode in a scintillant shower of blazing silver.

"Another event over," said Luden grimly. "Let us hope that the scores are remaining even."

An illuminated board gave the answer, lights flashing as they changed the figures on the panel. It was one of hundreds scattered throughout the city, only a few could actually see the events, most watched through monitors and relays in the telehouses. But all were interested in the shift of the aggregate points.

Tonight winners would drink to their luck, losers glowered over their form sheets.

"Oyte," said Kennedy. "Four points gained. Mhul two. Tavoy two. Terra unchanged."

"We need not have been competing," reminded Luden. "But we are certainly not in a favorable position. I am at a loss to understand how our predictions were so far out. We should have been holding our own at third place—now we have fallen to fifth."

"The human element, Jarl."

"Even so, knowing the importance of gaining the trophy, I would have expected a better result. It could be that something has happened, Cap. I suggest that we waste no time in making an investigation."

Time which was running out. The journey had been long, the games already started, a dozen events over, and yet Kennedy did not increase his pace. Instead he slowed a little, watching, his eyes checking faces to either side, studying the reflections in shop windows as they passed. Windows filled with a variety of sporting goods, miniature trophies, the souvenirs and gimcrackery always to be found at such times in such places.

An excess of caution, perhaps, but Kennedy never

made the mistake of underestimating an enemy and to certain parties any visiting Terrans would be objects of suspicion.

He slowed still more, finally halting before a window filled with boxes of confections; small cakes crusted with nuts, sweetmeats of a score of varieties, twists of spun sugar, crystals of pungent gums, things to suck and chew while watching the screens. The center piece was a casket filled with succulent dainties, the lid containing a smoothly reflective mirror.

The man he had spotted earlier had halted across the street.

He was thin, wiry, with eyes which were closely set and hands which held glitters at their tips. He wore a neat dress of tunic and pants of a semi-military style. His hair was dyed, roached, a yellow crest over a peaked skull. His mouth held pointed teeth which gnawed at his lower lip.

He was a Gillelian, and Kennedy knew of their penchant for assassination.

Quietly he said, "Jarl, go into the shop. Be casual. Once inside look through the window. The Gillelian opposite could have company."

Kennedy moved, casual as he inspected the displayed wares, watching as Luden's face appeared at the window, a girl at his side, his finger pointing to a box of brightly colored gums. His nod was more than an agreement to accept the price.

The Gillelian was alone then, or if he had a companion he wasn't close. Luden's view, better than his own, would have scanned the street. Kennedy moved on, his senses keened to a sharp alertness. He rounded the next corner, stepped quickly for a few yards then slowed, stooping as if to pick something off the ground, a quick backward glance revealing the Gillelian now on his side of the street and close.

A coincidence, perhaps, but Kennedy had long since learned to trust his instincts when it came to danger. The man had followed them for too long after they had left the others. He could have been set on watch, primed with instructions, paid to kill.

And, if paid, he would carry out his bargain. To a Gillelian it was a matter of pride and personal honor.

He came a little closer, his face blank, one hand lifting as if to scratch his cheek. A casual wanderer killing time, maybe, out for a little air, one of a number lost in the crowd.

A crowd that was thin here in the side street and would be thinner farther from the main avenue.

Kennedy walked on, counting steps, judging time, distance and opportunity. A woman approached and he watched her eyes, the sway of her body as she moved to glide past him, the man who now had to be very close.

Three more steps and Kennedy spun, seeing the lifted hand, the glint of metal at the tips of the fingers. Needle-pointed steel smeared with poison—a prick and he would be dead.

The upsweep of his left arm hit the threat an inch from his eyes, knocking the tips up and to his left as his right hand, the fingers bent at the second knuckle, drove forward like the piston of an engine. It hit low on the throat, crushing cartilage, impacting vital nerves, stunning, killing.

A woman cried out as the Gillelian slumped, her eyes round, shocked, the cry turning to a gasp of concern as Kennedy caught the falling body, supporting it, careful of the hands, the poisoned nails.

"What—is he ill?"

She had seen a blur of motion and was already doubting the evidence of her eyes. The hands reaching had obviously been to help, not hurt. The blow had made little sound and the blood which would have welled from the mouth was trapped beneath Kennedy's clamping hand.

He said, quickly, "Don't wory about it, madam. My friend has had a little too much to drink. You understand—a lucky win, he insisted on celebrating."

His face, his voice, tempted her to linger. Such things

happened, a casual meeting, a little common ground and then, perhaps, romance.

Then, reluctantly, she changed her mind. There were too many years between them. Had she been ten years younger things could have been different.

"Are you sure he'll be all right? I could summon a guard and he'll send for an ambulance."

"Thank you, no." Kennedy turned the head a little, conscious of the wetness of his hand. He heard the sound of running feet and Luden was suddenly beside him, blocking the woman's view.

"You've found him," he said. "Good. Our hotel is just around the corner." To the woman he said, "Thank you for your concern, madam, but I assure you that it isn't necessary. We can do all that needs to be done."

A cultured, slightly odd, but obviously respectable man. And it was growing late, the streets becoming even more crowded, and she wanted to get home.

As she walked away, Kennedy said, "Your handkerchief, Jarl. My hand."

The fabric covered the stain, a narrow opening, filled with deepening gloom, swallowed the body. As lights flared from the standards to replace the crimson glow of the sun, a rocket threw emerald fire into the sky to signal the ending of yet another event.

And Terra had dropped another place.

CHAPTER
SIX

"I can't understand it, Cap. We should be winning, not hitting the skids."

Carl Devaney paced the floor of his room. He was a wizened monkey of a man, his eyes like splintered marbles, his body made of string and wire. Any of his team could have broken him with one hand—but they were what he had made them.

Devaney had picked the trainers, the coaches, determined the diets, the exercises, taking bone and flesh and muscle and turning it into a machine designed to do one thing better than anyone else.

A fanatic, but no manager of a successful team could be anything else. And Devaney was the best.

Pausing, he said, "We should have won the discus. The long-jump was ours until we went on the field. The hundred-sprint, the high-jump, the caber—damn it, Cap. How could I have been so wrong?"

"You managed to get points, Carl."

"Points, yes, but not the bonus." Davaney resumed his pacing. "Take Lammelech. He's the best javelin thrower I've come across. He should have won tonight—instead he just made the last place."

Luden said, "Was his distance normal?"

"No, Jarl. He didn't meet his own preliminary standard. Don't ask me why."

"Who else should we ask?" Kennedy was cold. "You're in charge here, Carl. You've got the authority and so can't escape the responsibility. And you know what's at stake. Did you question Lammelech?"

"Naturally. He was downbeat, said he had done his best and didn't want to talk about it. That's natural, Cap; these athletes are like delicate watches with overwound springs. A word, a look even, can throw them off. Commanding a MALACA is child's play to handling a bunch of temperamental highly strung specialists. I've worn myself thin trying to maintain their peak." Devaney added, bitterly, "It looks as if I've failed."

"Yes." Kennedy had neither the time nor the inclination to feed the man lies or comfort. "The point is are you going to continue to fail? What is your assessment of the position?"

"Bad." Devaney halted beside a small table bearing a decanter and goblets. He poured himself a drink and swallowed it at a gulp. "We're too far down the list, Cap. If Cho'loctacol and Vaney hadn't pulled out for some reason, we wouldn't stand a chance."

Weit's doing and his efforts mustn't be allowed to go to waste.

Kennedy strode to the window and stood looking at the night. The Terran camp occupied a portion of a soaring building which curved to embrace the oval of the stadium; a miniature fortress in which the teams were jealously guarded each in their own suites, the athletes attended by their trainers, attendants and managers. A hundred entrants—five thousand people with at least a thousand local guards.

The guards didn't matter, the trainers and managers now had little to do aside from maintaining morale, the crux of the problem was the contenders themselves.

Turning, Kennedy said, "Split the team. Those who have already participated must be kept from those who have yet to enter."

Devaney frowned. "I don't like it, Cap. They have grown pretty close and it could play hell with their spirit. The losers did their best."

"Which wasn't good enough!"

"But—"

"It is a matter of contamination, Carl," said Luden thinly. "Those who have lost will tend, subconsciously, to affect the others. They will not want to be shown up and revealed as the failures they know themselves to be. If the others also lose then they will have maintained their prestige. Cap is right, those who have yet to perform must be isolated from the others."

"I still don't like it."

"Then lump it." Kennedy was curt. "How about discipline, after a contender has participated he relaxes a little, right?"

"Of course."

"And so lowers the standard. Do as I say, Carl. And another thing. Feed them nothing but what you take from sealed cans and bottles."

Devaney's annoyance vanished as he understood what Kennedy was driving at. For a moment he stood in thought, then firmly shook his head.

"It isn't possible, Cap. Those contenders couldn't have been drugged. That's one thing I can swear to."

"And can you be certain that an attempt won't be made?" Kennedy didn't wait for an answer. "This is war, Carl, and the sooner you and the team realize it the better. Real war with Earth itself at stake. We can't afford to take the slightest chance."

Back at the window he studied the exterior of the building. The walls were sheer, broken only by carvings depicting events in the games. The windows were unbarred and their catches simple.

A natural oversight—the interior of the building was patrolled, the corridors guarded, doors firmly locked. Nothing but a fly could have scaled the walls and only an invisible fly could have hoped to escape being spotted by the moving circles of light which continually traced paths over the stone. Searchlights operated from towers at the edge of the stadium and manned by local guards.

The arena itself was blazing with a wash of brilliance, clustered figures small as they vied with each other. The events were continuous, the seats always filled, the scanners always busy.

"Marksmanship." said Devaney from Kennedy's side. "This one's going to be close."

"Have we participated yet?"

"No—we go down in a few minutes. I should be there. Hamill's a good man but he's a little on edge."

He stood in the annex of the suite, a tall man with a

thin figure and hollow cheeks. His eyes were a pale blue and his hands were those of an artist, slender, finely boned. Not an athlete in the accepted sense of the word, but a specialist who had trained himself to be as near-perfect as a machine in the pursuit of a single skill.

That of placing a bullet exactly where he wanted it to go.

His rifle was a Quain-Special, firing a 6mm slug, bolt operated, built with the fine precision of a watch. The slugs were standard calibre for the competition as the gun was the standard weapon.

Kennedy glanced at it, but made no effort to touch it, noting instead the individual touches, the raised comb of the stock, the extra cushioning at the butt. Small things but they would help the man to become a part of the weapon, the rifle an extension of his being.

A girl stood at his side, Lynne Bailey, a swimmer who moved with a liquid grace which disguised the overdevelopment of the muscles of calves and thighs.

"Cap!" She smiled as Devaney made the introduction. "I've heard of you. You walked off with the trophy at the Usag Aquatics, right?"

"I was lucky."

"You were a damned good swimmer," she corrected. "If you'd worked at it you'd have been on the team now instead of me."

"Perhaps, but I had other things to do."

"Such as?" She shook her head as he made no reply, a somewhat plain girl with a broad face and short hair, eyes which held a bleached hazel, the touch of distant horizons. "All right, Cap, I can guess. Too busy enjoying yourself to get down to hard work. You've met Boyd?"

"I have now." Kennedy touched his hand. Boyd Cannon, an expert with the sword, yet to prove his skill in the games.

"And Cayne?"

Cayne was the obstacle runner, a taut mass of nerve and sinew, his mouth twisted in a perpetual sneer.

He said, "What is this—old home week?"

"So what if it is?" A blocky man came toward them from an inner room. He had red hair, a freckled face and bulky shoulders. "Hi, Cap. I'm Sean Fahey. I used to have a brother."

A man who had died in a horrible way—how horrible Sean would never know if Terran Control had anything to do with it.

"He was a good man," said Kennedy.

"The best."

"And you?" Kennedy met the vivid blue eyes. "You'll be racing soon, are you going to win?"

"You're damned right I'm going to win! You too, Cayne, and you, Lynne. We're all going to win. How about it, Sam?"

Hamill said, "I shall do my best."

"Best—hell!" Sean's voice was a snarl. "You're going to damn well win! Come back without a first and I'll smash your hands!"

"Sean! That's enough!" Devaney stepped between the two men. "You should be resting, get to it!"

"Am I a child?"

"You're the member of the Terran team and you'll do what I say or you'll get the hell out of here!" Small though he was Carl Devaney dominated the assembly, a demonstration of the spirit and drive which had made him what he was. "I mean it, Sean. You know that."

"I know it." Sean drew in his breath and Kennedy knew that the man, despite his apparent bombast, was poised on the edge of an emotional storm.

Devaney nodded when, after the man had gone, Kennedy mentioned it.

"I know, Cap. He took the death of his brother hard and now this competition has become something personal to him. A way to get revenge. It could help if he doesn't let his anger get the better of him."

A risk which Kennedy would have preferred not to take. Rage, at times, could be a help, but never when at the wheel of a racing car traveling in a cluster of others on a rough circuit at around three hundred miles an hour.

Nor would it help a man to hit a tiny target at three hundred yards.

As the group passed from the annex into the outside corridor Kennedy studied the marksman with professional interest. Kennedy could shoot and had proved his skill often—without it he would have been long since dead and others with him. But he had not devoted hours a day for years on end to gain that particular ability. And Hamill would not be shooting at targets which could shoot back.

It made a difference.

At his side, Luden said quietly, "I do not think this is wise, Cap. I can appreciate the desire of Hamill to have the presence of friends nearby while he is competing, yet it exposes them to potential danger."

A possibility Kennedy had considered, yet to have objected would have been to erode Devaney's authority. And there was need for discretion. Athletes talked among themselves and traveled widely. A sharp ear might pick up gossip and a shrewd brain wonder just who and what Kennedy was.

Questions he preferred not to be asked.

Superficially he was a dilettante who had come to indulge his hobby and who had used influence to get close to the team. Luden was his advisor and mentor—a facade which they had adopted often before. Devaney had spread the word before they had arrived—only he knew of Kennedy's real purpose and even then he knew nothing of the details.

And it seemed safe enough. The corridor led to an elevator, guarded, to a lower level, also guarded, to an underground passage leading to the stadium which was thick with more guards.

Even so Kennedy remained alert as the party headed down the underground passage, Lynne at Hamill's side, Cayne and Cannon to their rear, Devaney himself trotting ahead like a questing hound.

At the contenders entrance he paused and said, "I'll

take Sam in and check him through. The rest of you had better find some seats."

But not in the public enclosures. A section had been reserved for contenders and privileged visitors and Kennedy sat with Luden on the tier behind the others. A spot which gave them a good view.

Not that there was much to be seen. The marksmen were in individual booths, sections shielded one from the other by plastic partitions. The targets were far in the distance, signals flashing over each after every shot, an illuminated panel showing individual scores.

Hamill was doing well. Lying prone on the ground, body at an angle to the line of fire, legs parted a little, elbows firmly set, he shot with a calm sureness. Automatically he used techniques which had become a part of his nature: to breathe evenly, to empty his chest as he took aim, to hold the rifle firm against cheek and shoulder, to squeeze the trigger gently.

To send bullet after bullet smashing into the bull's-eye.

"We should win this one." Devaney was grimly confident. "Hamill's in top form."

A conviction Kennedy didn't share. Oyote and Guisa were also doing well. Muhl would fire later as would a dozen others, Tavoy among them. Even a hundred percent score at this time was no surety of gaining a first—ties would have to be reshot.

Kennedy felt a sharp tingle on his wrist: the attention signal from the disguised communicator he wore. Casually he lifted his hand as if to note the time, then pulled thoughtfully at the lobe of his left ear.

Saratov's voice was a thin whisper. "Ready to go, Cap."

He and Chemile had found a room close to the stadium, an elementary precaution against capture or discovery. No one could connect either of them with the Terran team.

Kennedy whispered, "Give it another thirty minutes, Penza. Jarl will mark the Terran window. You've spotted where to go?"

"Yes. The lights?"

"I'll do what I can."

Kennedy rose, stretching, a spectator who had seen enough. Luden caught his eye and joined him.

Carl Devany glanced at his watch. "I guess we'd better all turn in. Come on, Boyd."

Cayne said. "Not me. It's early yet."

"Don't be awkward!" Lynne Bailey was sharp. "Once you've won your event you can do as you like, but now you should cooperate. Right, Carl?"

Devaney thinned his lips. "Listen, Cayne," he snapped. "You heard what I said to Sean. That goes for you too. I want no rebels on this team and don't give me any guff about how grown up you are. Now, on your feet and move!"

Cayne hesitated as if inclined to argue, then, looking upwards, he saw Kennedy's face over the manager's shoulder.

He said quickly, "All right. You don't have to look at me like that. I'm coming."

Luden had gone.

He wandered toward the searchlight towers, a man careless of time who wanted to see the sights. A watching guard saw nothing suspicious, curiosity was not a crime, and the last thing Luden looked was a man intent on sabotage.

Within a few minutes he had decided that the towers were fed with power from a common source—an unexpected bonus. Mentally he traced the underground wiring to the point where that source had to be. Electrical engineers worked on a basis of cold logic when it came to fitting installations and, while aesthetics demanded that the equipment be buried so as not to offend the eye, economy dictated the least expensive installation.

For a moment he stood, hands in his pockets, then scuffing the ground with the toe of his shoe, he wandered on.

The scuff had covered the small device he had let fall; a low-powered directional bomb fitted with a time fuse. Detonating it would vent its force downward against the buried junction.

At the entrance to the underground passage there was trouble.

A man stood arguing with a guard, a big man who waved his arms and shouted, his voice rising above the sharp crackle of shots from the marksmen.

"Damn it, I've the right! I belong to the Cho'loctacol!"

"Your team has been withdrawn, sir," said the guard patiently. "You are no longer entitled to use this passage. Neither should you be in this area."

"To hell with that! I want to get back to my old room. I've forgotten something valuable."

"If you will present yourself to the main entry, arrangements can be made. But this passage is reserved for the use of contenders only."

"You—"

The man, glowering, struck at the guard who avoided the fist with a deft movement. As his attacker stumbled, thrown off balance by the force of his own blow, the guard grabbed at his arm.

"He's too weak," sneered Cayne. "He should have used his Dione." He pressed forward into the small crowd that had gathered. "Hit him!" he yelled. "Knock the fool senseless!"

There was no need. Other guards came running, among them a vendor of delicacies balancing his heavy tray. Kennedy watched him, aware of something wrong. Such a man would avoid trouble, not run toward it. He looked to his side, Lynne Bailey stood with Devaney, Cannon a little to their rear, a few others around. If the man with the tray should fall—

"Away!" Kennedy lunged at the girl, hit her, his shoulder slamming against the muscle of her back. "Cannon! Run!"

The warning came too late. As the girl staggered forward and fell, the vendor reached the low parapet separating the reserved area from the seats above. For a moment he seemed to hang suspended in the air, then was falling, the heavy tray leaving his hands to hurtle like a bullet landing where Cannon stood.

Automatically he threw up his right arm.

"Damn!" Devaney's voice rose above the din. "Boyd, are you hurt? Boyd?"

An accident, as a dozen witnesses would swear. A vendor of trifles losing his balance and suffering minor hurt to his body—the complete loss of his stock.

An accident—but Boyd Cannon had a broken right arm!

CHAPTER
SEVEN

To the patroling guards Penza Saratov was just another of the nuisances common during the games. He weaved and sang and staggered a little, a grotesquely fat man dressed in loose robes, the moon of his face wreathed in an idiot smile.

"A challenge!" he bawled. "I'll challenge any man to a fight. Any two men." He peered at the guards. "Wanna take me on?"

"Not tonight, sir." The guard leader had a sharp eye; the robes were of expensive material and the fat man could have influence or friends in high places. In any case he was doing little harm even though he was close to the team-building.

"When then?" Saratov staggered and came to rest against the stone of the facade. Above his head circles of light weaved their brilliant tracery. "They wouldn't let me enter," he complained, waving toward the stadium. "Wouldn't let me make the team. The best fighter on Hemph—no wonder they lost."

"You'll make it the next time."

"Maybe." Saratov blinked and slumped, sliding down with his back against the wall. "They wouldn't take me," he muttered. "Ten thousand decals lost, but that I can afford. But pride—Hemph will never be the same after this."

"Maybe we should take him in," suggested a guard. "It would be for his own good." Stepping forward he gripped Saratov's arm and heaved. "Hell, he's heavy!"

Too heavy, decided the leader.

"He's out and can do no harm. We'll keep an eye on him and watch that he doesn't get robbed." There was small chance of that in this protected area. "Give him a few hours and then we'll get him on his feet and back

61

home. There could be a bonus in it for those who take the trouble."

"Us," said one of his men. "We'll do it when going off-duty."

The leader nodded, glancing at his watch. "That'll be in—" He broke off as a dull report echoed from the stadium. "The lights!"

The searchbeams had died, the facade of the building now illuminated only by a diffuse glow from a line of floods, a light which threw the lower section into sharp relief but which dimmed rapidly into a pearly haze.

The guard leader knew his job.

"Scatter—random patrol," he snapped. "Watch for intruders. Move!"

Saratov stirred as he heard the thud of retreating boots. Rising, he moved past the row of floodlights, eyes searching the relative gloom.

"Veem?"

A portion of the ground moved, rose to take the shape of a man.

"We'll have to make this fast," said the giant. "Those guards are no fools."

Chemile was already at work. From a bag which had lain hidden beneath him he took geccko pads, slipping them on his elbows, his wrists, ankles, and knees. A flat pouch hugged his stomach, held by suction.

"The Terran window, spotted it?" Saratov grunted as Chemile nodded. "Good. Ready now?"

"Quit talking and let's see some action."

The giant grunted again. He stepped behind Chemile, gripped and tensed.

"Now!"

His muscles exploded in a violent burst of energy, his entire body converted into a spring which uncoiled with sufficient force to send Chemile flying up and toward the building. He hit, slipped a little, then as the pads held his weight, apparently vanished.

Saratov slumped as the guards returned.

"That man? Where—" The leader released his breath

in a sigh of relief as he spotted the huge bulk. "Here he is. Must have staggered then fallen again. Well, he was heading away from the building not toward it. Check for footprints while I try to rouse him."

Flower beds ran along the foot of the facade, the soft dirt broken only where Saratov had sat, unmarked aside from the single line of prints he had left.

He mumbled as the guard leader shook his arm.

"Wha— wassa matter?"

"Up!" The man was insistent. "On your feet, sir. You should not be here."

He heaved and Saratov climbed groggily to his feet.

"Tired," he said. "I wanna go home. Help me home. I'll pay." A big hand dived into a pocket and returned loaded with coins. "Get me a cab, uh? I feel terrible."

From high overhead where he clung to the smooth stone of the wall, Chemile looked downward as the giant was led away. A good performance, but he had to do as well and his part was the most difficult. First to climb, then to find the right windows, to get into the various suites and do what had to be done.

The killing of the searchlights had helped, even if blended into the background movement and the shift of shadows could have betrayed him. Now he had to move fast before the lights were repaired.

It wasn't easy. The wall was sheer and only two of the pads could be released at any one time. It was a matter of establishing a rhythm; release, move, clamp, release, move clamp, leg after arm, arm after leg. Within minutes he felt the ache of muscles, the drag of sinews. The decorations were a problem, they had to be avoided and that meant sidling along the wall. Windows too had to be given a wide berth, at any moment someone could open one and look outside.

And he had to remember every foot of the way, using the marked window as a guide, counting levels as he moved upwards.

He tensed as to his left a wide circle suddenly blazed with light, one of the towers had been put back into operation. The beam sliced across the wall and he froze as it hit him, moving up quickly as it passed, freezing again as it returned.

Worried, the guards were making a quick check of the building, any ordinary interloper would have been discovered.

Chemile halted to one side of a window, then moved cautiously toward it. It was dark, the curtains drawn back, the glimmer of a reflection like a pale ghost in the interior of the room. It came from a disc of bright metal, the surface engraved with the Zheltyana Seal, the ancient sign of convoluted interwound circles which was thought by many races to bring good fortune. A vigil light stood before it, the tiny flame a steady beacon. It guttered as Chemile opened the window, the catch sprung by a flexible strip of steel. Slipping into the room he closed the window behind him and stood for a moment, listening.

He heard a sigh, the shift of a moving body, a snore.

Safely tucked away in a high level of the building the Oyte team had settled down for the night.

Chemile removed the pads and stuck them to his back together with the flat pouch. If discovered they wouldn't betray him by ruining his camouflage. A door opened beneath his hand revealing a chamber flanked by other doors, the figure of a man asleep in a chair.

The night attendant of the team.

He was thin, his arms long, his face resembling that of a koala bear, the ears high and pointed, the snout a ball over the lipless mouth. From the pouch at his rear Chemile took a vial, held it beneath the nose and touched a stud.

The spray was silent, colorless, odorless, would leave no trace but made certain that the man wouldn't wake for at least the next hour.

Time enough to do what had to be done.

Like a ghost, Chemile flitted from room to room, fitting faces to remembered photographs. Most he ignored, over some he hovered, touching skins with drugs which were immediately absorbed, using the sleep-spray on any restless figure.

Sealed bottles stood on a table in a room holding a rubbing couch. Vials of tonic and lotions to tone skin and muscle. With a hypodermic needle Chemile added a few drops to each through the seals, the minute punctures unnoticeable.

Satisfied, he made a final check then headed back toward the room holding the shrine.

The first team taken care of and now only six to go.

He wondered if Luden was having similar success.

Luden was playing chess.

The Argh of Tavoy was a fanatic on the game. He sat on a padded chair before which rested a low table bearing a board made of silver and gold. A small wizened man with a snub nose and prominent front teeth, he held some of the appearance of a rabbit, but there was nothing rabbitlike about either him or his team.

"It is good of you to accommodate an old man at his simple pleasure," he said as Luden took his place. "I was most gratified to learn of your presence on Regak. A casual visit?"

But far from a casual question. Luden glanced at the others assembled in the main room of the Tavoyan suite. Garz Aist was wealthy and it showed. He had taken double accommodation and had imported his own furnishings. Grills had been fitted over the interiors of all windows, his personal guards maintained an armed watch, even his servants carried the heavy knives of tradition.

And he was generous in entertainment. Wine had flowed together with tempting dainties; spiced cakes and compots of succulent fruits, sweetmeats and comfits of fifty kinds. His guests, dilettantes from a dozen worlds, had eaten and drunk well. Now they clustered about the area where he sat before the chessboard.

An old man, shrewd, cunning with the skill of long years of arduous diplomacy. A man who, somehow, had to be persuaded to become Earth's friend.

He smiled as Luden nodded in answer to the question.

"The games," he said. "A wonderful spectacle, as I think you will agree. Worlds competing against each other—I cannot resist taking a personal interest. And now to the game? You wish some refreshment before we begin? No? Then let us decide the first move."

The pieces were of emerald and ruby. Luden picked up a pawn of each, manipulated them behind his back then held out his closed hands. Eyes of mottled agate studied his face as the Argh reached a thin hand toward them. It drifted toward the left, hesitated, moved to the right and then, like a striking bird of prey, moved back to the left to lower, to touch like a falling leaf.

"It is your first move, my lord." Luden replaced the pieces, his face impassive. He had forced the choice with a carefully calculated flicker of his eyes. The gain was small, but the final victory could depend on such accumulations.

The game commenced. Garz Aist moved slowly, lingering as if undecided, pursing his lips and frequently tugging at the lobe of his right ear. Luden moved with quick precision, acting as though he followed a previously conceived plan. Both men lied with every move they made. The Argh had no need to act like a fumbling beginner and Luden had no plan. He could play the game and play it well, but he was not playing simple chess. He was playing against a man who played chess, a small but important difference.

"A fascinating game," murmured Garz Aist. "If nothing else good ever came from Earth, the game of chess would ensure that the world would never be forgotten. At my palace I have a thousand sets; men carved from ivory, from bone, from metal and made of seeds. Boards of as many materials, some of them decorated with fantastic designs. One day you must see them." He moved a piece, removed another. "You were careless, my friend. Already you are weakened."

Luden moved without comment.

"I hear there was trouble at the stadium. An accident."

"Yes."

"One of your team injured?"

"Yes." Luden moved a bishop. "But not seriously, I hope."

"As do I." The Argh sucked at his teeth as he studied the board. "A cruel mischance if it costs you the trophy. Sometimes fate can be most unkind."

Luden made no comment, concentrating on the board. The pattern which had developed was almost classical and would lead to his inevitable defeat. He must break it, shatter the attack and launch an offensive. Not a neat textbook series of moves which could be matched and countered, but a blasting away threatening pieces and the opening out of the game. Not chess as he would have liked it, perhaps, but good survival tactics.

"You know," said the Argh as the game progressed, "I have often thought this to be a game with far wider implications than most players realise. Take the men we move. Isn't it true that, in a way, we control their destiny? We save them, sacrifice them, use them as we will. Suppose they had individual awareness—can you accept the premise?"

Luden moved a rook and took a knight. He lost the attacking piece and at once took a pawn which had posed no immediate threat but which he won without cost. An error on the part of Garz Aist. Or an apparent error. Luden reminded himself that the man, while no master, was far from being an amateur.

He studied the board, feeling a sharpened interest at the challenge to his intelligence. He did not have the dedication necessary to achieve the highest quality of play, but he did have the ability to summarize a problem in terms of elementary components. And the Argh was one of those components.

"Men moved on a cosmic board," mused Garz Aist. He had stopped tugging at his ear. "Units at the mercy of an unknown player. There is a religious sect, I believe, which has incorporated that concept into its credo."

"The Nyeed of Lynac." Luden moved a bishop. "Your move, my lord."

He had forced the play and immediately launched his attack.

"We all have delusions of grandeur. The desire to simplify a complex world into the neat pattern of a chess board, with ourselves, naturally, as the players, never the pawns. Adults leave such fantasies in the realm of childhood where they belong. A few cling to the notion as do the Nyeed as compensation for their own inadequacy. Vicious rulers, also, as an excuse to justify reprehensible deeds. If we are pieces manipulated on a board then the player, not ourselves, must be responsible for all that we do. Your move, my lord."

He gave the man no time to think. As the thin hand hovered over the board he said, "The concept holds no merit and never has. Belief in an omnipotent being is no excuse for vile actions. A man, if he is a man, must accept the responsibility for what he does. A friend, betrayed, is living proof of the perfidy of the betrayer."

The Argh moved, making a bad mistake. Luden swept up the exposed piece.

Fifteen minutes later he knew that he had won.

The game was not yet over, but like a list of familiar equations the end result was clear. Luden sat back in his chair, relaxing a little. Idly he looked around.

The room was almost full.

Others had joined the initial group, high officials from the various teams, invited as Luden had been invited to the party. An unusual event, but Garz Aist was an unusual man. A complex character whose background had caused the crew of the *Mordain* long hours of careful study. An absolute ruler of a small collection of worlds with chess his overriding hobby.

The node which Kennedy had decided opened a field of attack. A common meeting ground in which he and his opponent would gain some small affinity. Luden's prowess at chess had been carefully broadcast, the invitation was inevitable.

Now he had to make the most of it.

To win?

To gain the other's respect at having bested him on

his own terms? But Earth needed the Argh as a friend and such a man, publicly humiliated, might gain a later revenge.

Luden studied the man where he sat. Garz Aist seemed to have shrunk a little, one finger now riding at the side of the snub nose, the hand a mask for the lips beneath. The eyes too were a mask, emotionless, unseeing, yet aware of the watchers. The men and women who had taken his bounty would relish his defeat.

They shifted a little, met Luden's stare, held it for a long, intense moment.

Luden said quietly, "If I may impose on your generosity, my lord? A glass of wine?"

The finger fell away from the nose, and the eyes widened a little. Then they were once again a mask. Yet something had left the small figure perched on the padded chair. Fear, perhaps? Tension, certainly.

"Wine, my friend? But of course. Persh, fetch a bottle of the finest vintage."

An attendant obeyed the signal of the lifted hand, the thin fingers bright with gems. The wine was cool, sweet, refreshing to the tongue. Luden sipped, then swallowed. Now, his decision made, he could afford to relax. Yet even so the game had to be played out to the end. It was not enough to lose, he had to make it appear that he fought every step of the way.

Garz Aist said, "It is your move, I think."

Luden lifted a piece, set it down. "Check."

A simple check, easy to block. A skilled player would notice the mistake, not obviously bad, but one which gave an advantage. Five moves, he thought, nine at the most. The Argh would have reason to boost his victory.

It took seven, a happy compromise.

CHAPTER
EIGHT

The voices were whispers in an orange haze.

"It goes well, brother."

"Very well, sister. I am almost tempted to take a personal interest."

"That would be unfair."

"Fairness? What is that?"

The sound of alien mirth, whispering tinkles which could have been the echoes of laughter or of water cascading over rocks, splintered ice showering, metal grating beneath a file.

Kennedy stirred, waking, yet the dream persisted.

A place of orange mist in which strange shapes moved in unexpected directions. Amorphous things which held no recognizable form and yet contained hints of disturbing familiarity. A sense of movement coupled with the conviction of stasis. An alien something which touched the core of his mind and froze even as it burned.

The nightmares of delirium.

The presence of the Sukhi.

Again he heard the voices, whispers scratching the surface of his brain. Ants beneath his skull.

"The challenge holds unanticipated factors, sister. These things provide much amusement. A personal wager?"

"Of what, brother?"

"A term of yavani. Take a side. If they win the contest—"

"You will pay me, brother. I am intrigued. There is a strong mind at work. Raise your perception to the elphos region, concentrate, you note?"

"A determination to survive. But wait, sister, others have different ideas."

Again the sound of mirth, alien, horrible.

Not horrible—different.

Different and frightening.

70